For Charlie, who is gentle and loving; for Max, who I know will be good
and kind like his dad; and for Thomas, who started all this.
- LA

For Sam, the best boy I know!
And for Lauren, who brought me along on this adventure!
- JL

Rey

Nattie

Bobby

Tam

MIX
Paper from
responsible sources
FSC® C104723

The Forest Stewardship Council® (FSC®) is an international, non-governmental organisation
dedicated to promoting responsible management of the world's forests. FSC operates a
system of forest certification and product labelling that allows consumers to identify wood
and wood-based products from well-managed forests and other controlled sources.

For more information about the FSC, please visit their website at www.fsc.org

LiTTLE TiGER
LONDON
CATERPILLAR BOOKS
An imprint of the Little Tiger Group • www.littletiger.co.uk
1 Coda Studios, 189 Munster Road, London SW6 6AW • Imported into the EEA
by Penguin Random House Ireland, Morrison Chambers, 32 Nassau Street,
Dublin D02 YH68 • First published in Great Britain 2021
Text copyright © Lauren Ace 2021 • Illustrations copyright © Jenny Løvlie 2021
A CIP catalogue record for this book is available from the British Library
All rights reserved • Printed in China • ISBN: 978-1-83891-159-1
CPB/1400/1878/0621 • 4 6 8 10 9 7 5 3

The Boys

Lauren Ace   Jenny Løvlie

Our story starts by the shore,
with four boys bobbing on the sea.

The boys had been friends for as long as they could remember,
and a little while before that. They were like brothers.

They all had different ways of expressing themselves.

Tam made art...   ...from everything.

They all loved listening
to Rey make music.

Nattie never went anywhere without a book
and often told them stories of his own.

Bobby liked to understand how things worked
and enjoyed explaining what he had found.

Although they all had different interests, the boys were a team.
When they worked together it made all of them better.

The beach was their special place. It was their playground...

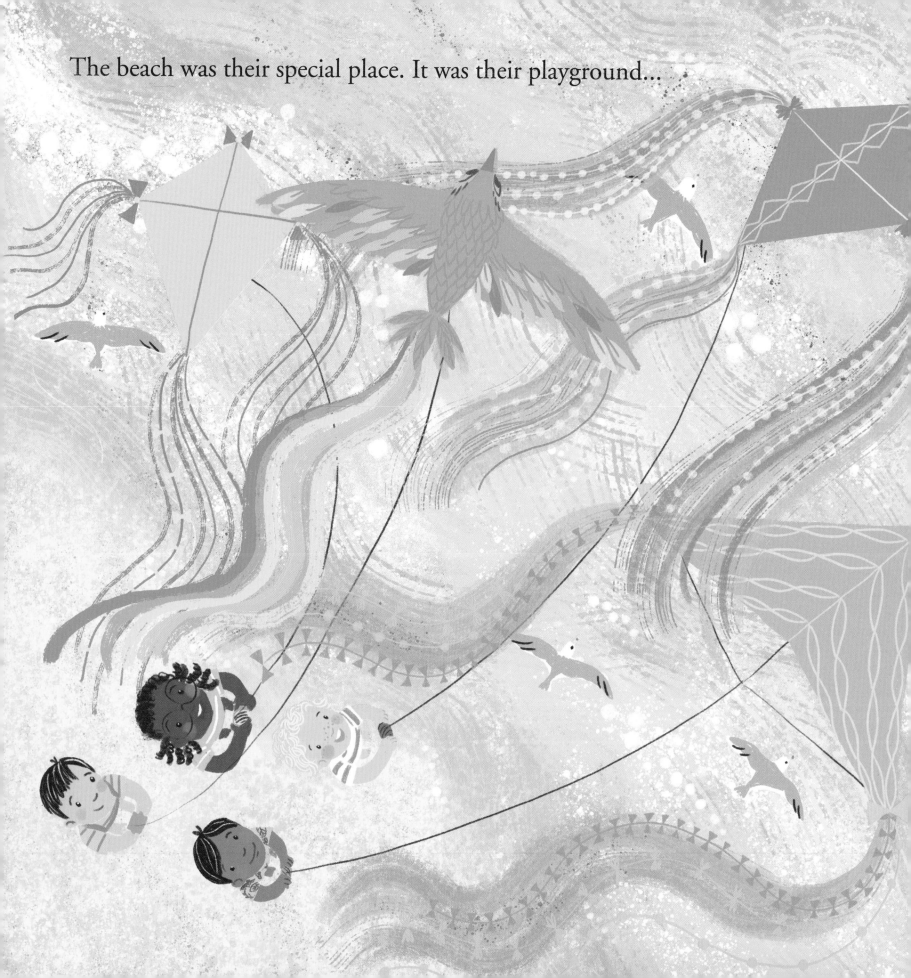

...their classroom...

...their second home.

It was where they
built their friendship.

Even when they weren't all together, the boys' lives were busy and full.

Of friends, family, hobbies and responsibilities.

But one spring they returned to their beach to find the sands had shifted.
The winter tides and storms had revealed hidden rocks and everything was different.

Sometimes, the boys found that growing up wasn't easy.

They had always stuck together and faced
competition as a team, but as they got older they
began to compete with one another.

Bobby and Nattie both wanted to be top of the class;
neither was very good at coming second.

Rey, who was usually the peacekeeper,
began to put other relationships before his friends.

Tam's jokes, which usually made their
hearts feel lighter, were no longer just for them.
Lately, he was entertaining larger crowds.

For a little while the boys enjoyed standing out on their own.

It felt good to be different and think only about what made them happy.

But without the others, each of the boys soon felt as though he had been swept out to sea.

Their successes, which had once been shared, now felt empty.

The boys knew they had to be able to talk about their feelings...

...but it wasn't easy.

Just as they had when they were small,
the friends worked together to make things better.

They came to realise that no boy is an island and the
bravest way to face problems is to talk and to listen.

They learned to be patient and kind with one another again,
making their friendship stronger than ever.

The boys became men and started families of their own.

When one of them was weighed down by sadness,
the others would always be there to lift him up.

The men understood that storms didn't last forever;
a bright new beginning would always follow.

And although their lives had taken them to different places,
the men came back together to share their happiest times.

The older they grew, the less the men
took their brotherhood for granted.

They knew that their friendship would always bring them back together,
just like waves returning to the shore.